CONTENT

CW00847656

PINKY SPINKS

CHAPTER ONE

Pinky Spinks made scrumptious sweets! Her most popular sweets were, Grinning Gobstoppers, Shocking Choccy Wocs, Funky Fudge Bites and Amazing Melting Mallows.

She was descended from a long line of wizards and magicians and had the power to make MAGIC SWEETS! If you want to find out when and for whom she made these special sweets, you will need to read this book!

Pinky's full first name was Pamela-Imogen-Natasha-Katherine-Yolande. You wouldn't want to say all those names would you? So, she was called Pinky for short.

Pinky had just bought a small house in a little village. The house had a big bow window to the front of it in which Pinky could display her sweets. Part of the house was being made into a shop and would be finished soon.

Pinky was a chubby old lady, she had pink cheeks and twinkling eyes which only lost their twinkle when she was REALLY, REALLY cross! Also, she looked very CUDDLY. She was wearing a yellow and black striped dress and she looked like a busy bumble bee as she buzzed around putting her belongings away.

She went to fetch her old teapot which had big, pink roses on it. It was in her nature to love anything that was pink! She made some tea and sitting in her armchair she drank two whole cups of tea and ate two sticky buns.

She began to knit furiously for she was making a woolly coat for her cat Sidney to keep him warm. It was all the colours of the rainbow and it meant she could see him clearly when he was outside.

Just then, Sidney strolled into the sitting room and jumping up on Pinky's lap, he curled himself up and began to cat nap! Pinky had put a dish of Amazing Melting Mallows on a side table and she popped one into her mouth. Wow! The sweet was made to last for ages! It fizzed and whizzed in your mouth and when you least expected it, it went PUFF and disappeared!

Pinky began to feel tired. Before she went to bed she went outside to have one last look at her shop window. Above the window, the name of the shop, SPINKS SWEETS was written in higgledy-piggledy writing, just like Pinky's own writing.

Half an hour later, Pinky climbed up the stairs to her bedroom. Sidney curled up at the foot of her bed and began to purr loudly; this soon sent Pinky to sleep. She started dreaming about new names for her candies such as Liquory Lick Licks, Rainbow Rockets and Sherbert Sizzlers.

Soon, the shop would be open and what a surprise the children would get when they tasted Pinky's FANTABULOUS SWEETS!!

PINKY SORTS OUT TYRONE TIBBS

CHAPTER TWO

The day dawned bright and sunny when Pinky opened her sweet shop for the first time.

Although she didn't know how old she was, she did know that her birthday was February 14th, Valentine's Day and it was the 14th that day.

She had put lots of big, red heart-shaped balloons in the window with red streamers and red tinsel hearts scattered around. A big sign said;

YOU WILL FALL IN LOVE WITH SPINKS SWEETS!

She added more jars of sweets to the other jars already in the window and these included Happy Humbugs, Liquory Lick Licks, Moorish Mints, Rainbow Rockets and Grinning Gobstoppers. There were also brightly packaged sweets with labels that said 'Spinks Sweets.'

The whole week before she opened the shop, children of all ages had come to her shop, pressing their noses to the window as excited as little puppies with their juicy bones. They had pointed to the sweets they most wanted to buy and waved cheerfully to Pinky who could be seen bustling about as she prepared the shop for opening.

At 8.30 in the morning, Pinky dressed herself in her

best flowery dress (decorated with pink roses of course), put on her pink slippers adorned with pink pom poms and put her hair in a tidy bun into which she stuck a pink rose.

At nine o'clock on the dot, she opened the door and was almost knocked over by a rush of children who were chattering excitedly. Their mothers and fathers seemed to be just as excited as they had never had a sweet shop in the village before.

Pinky stood behind her counter and was just about to serve the first little girl when the shop door crashed back against the wall and a tall boy about sixteen years old, pushed into the front of the queue, at the same time, knocking the little girl over.

'Ere, you old bat,' he demanded. 'Give me one of them there Grinning Gobstoppers. Make sure it's a big one and be quick about it. I haven't got all day, you know.'

Pinky was shocked at his rudeness. She glared at the boy. 'Old bat, old bat!' she muttered to herself. 'Really! What a rude boy!'

Some of the mothers were clucking their teeth together, sounding like indignant hens and shaking their heads in disbelief. One mother was helping the little girl up.

'Just a minute,' Pinky said to the big boy. 'I've got a new batch of Grinning Gobstoppers in my kitchen and they are much bigger than those in the window.'

Pinky went into her kitchen. She selected a very

large gobstopper and then went into her workroom. There she put it into a machine that whirred and purred and coated the gobstopper with different kinds of magic dust.

Going back into the shop, Pinky said to the boy, 'There you are, one of my biggest gobstoppers. You can thank me for finding you the biggest one.'

'I ain't fanking you for nuffink, you old bat!'' he shouted as he went out of the shop.

'Goodness me!' remarked Pinky. Then she said to her next customer, 'Is that boy always as rude as that?'

'Oh yes!' answered the little girl who was next in line. 'His name is Tyrone Tibbs and he is very rude to everyone, even the teachers in our school.'

Pinky said no more but quickly began to serve the next customers.

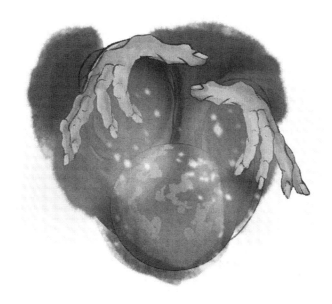

Meanwhile, outside the shop, Tyrone popped the Grinning Gobstopper into his mouth and could not believe how delicious it was. A big grin stole over his face and as he sucked the sweet his grin got BIGGER and BIGGER and BIGGER. Each time he tasted a new flavour he took the sweet out of his mouth to look at the new colour of it.

'Cor,' he said aloud. 'That old fuss-pot certainly knows how to make a good sweet.'

But then, he began to dribble a bit and when he next took the sweet out of his mouth he was sure it was larger than when he first tasted it.

He was halfway home when two of his school friends came along the street and waved to him from the other side of the road.

'Hey Tyrone, how are you doing?' called out one boy. 'Yeah,' added the other boy. ' Are you going to football later on? If so, we'll see you there.'

'Umph, aarg,' replied Tyrone. 'Mmfy bah ur gurr. Grrp ugh glug slurp. Glurp,slurp icky poo. Grrp,grrp glug glug.' Spitz y lar.' Tyrone's mouth was so puffed up with the Grinning Gobstopper he couldn't speak properly!

The two boys stared at him curiously, then shrugging their shoulders, they ran past him. It didn't do to upset Tyrone Tibbs!

Meanwhile Tyrone tried to pull the sweet out of his mouth with his fingers but it just would not budge! He began to panic.

'Tarj di ut bot,' he said out loud. 'Mmmph ga-ga. Umpy wumpy oof poof!'

He started to run home because he was worried he might meet some more friends and they might want to stop and talk to him. How could he speak to anyone when his mouth was gummed up with the sticky sweet!

By the time he reached home his mouth was so puffed out he looked like a warty toad! Fortunately, the rest of his family were out so he scribbled a note which said he wasn't feeling very well and leaving it on the kitchen table he went upstairs to his bedroom. When he looked in the mirror he couldn't believe what he saw. He looked like a monster in a horror film!

He began to see if he could get the sweet out by smacking his cheeks at the same time in the hope the sweet would fly out of his mouth, but no, the sweet would not budge!

Poor Tyrone spent most of the day in his room. He had to miss his football practice and was very bored by himself. Every now and then he got off his bed and looked in the mirror to see if he looked any better, but no, he just couldn't get rid of the sweet and it still puffed out his cheeks. In fact he was so bored he began to make up names for himself that matched his new appearance like Tyrone The Terrible or The Warty Wonder!

In the evening, he called downstairs to his mother to say he did not want any dinner although he was feeling really hungry.

Eventually, he fell asleep but he woke up early and wow! At last the sweet had disappeared! He went downstairs to eat his breakfast and was especially nice to his family. His brothers and sisters wondered what had happened to change Tyrone who was usually very grumpy in the morning.

Tyrone didn't visit Pinky's shop for a few weeks but when he did he asked politely for some Happy Humbugs; he never wanted to see a Grinning Gobstopper ever again!

CHAPTER THREE

Pinky had bought her shop in a small village. She liked the village because it had a clock tower overlooking a large green. There was a pond to one corner and in another corner, there was a play area with swings, slides, see-saws and roundabouts. To one side of the green there was a row of shops and on the other side was the village church with a little hall where parties and other events could be held. An open market was held on the green on Saturdays and Pinky decided she would like to set up a stall at the market to sell her sweets.

A few weeks after the grand opening of her shop, Pinky had become a bit of a celebrity in the village. The grown-ups began to call her Pinky although the children still called her Mrs. Spinks of course. She was often seen feeding the ducks, pushing children on the swings and of course everyone loved her scrumptious sweets! People began to ask her to help at fetes and to attend their children's parties.

One Monday morning it was raining heavily but Pinky didn't let it dampen her spirits. Oh no! She found on the front door mat an invitation to Millie Mason's birthday party on the following Saturday. She was to come along and bring some of her delicious sweets instead of buying a present for Millie.

Pinky was delighted with the invitation! She sat down to write an acceptance card and waited for the rain to stop to post her reply.

She was terribly excited as she loved parties but to keep her mind off it until the day of the party arrived she decided to do some decorating. Meanwhile, she thought about what she should wear for the party. She decided to wear something bright, colourful and trendy. And of course, whatever she chose would have to be PINK!! Pinky thought herself as something of a fashion guru!!

When Saturday arrived, Pinky dressed herself with care. She put on a pink and white striped top and a pair of pink spotted trousers. She tied her hair back with a pink spotted ribbon and then packed a large pink candy-striped straw bag with sweets and chocolates. She went and looked at herself in the bedroom mirror.

'I think I look very nice!' she said out loud. 'Yes, very nice indeed!' Then, leaving Sidney some tasty fish for his tea, she set out for Millie's party.

Millie's party was a great success! There was a magician who did lots of magic tricks. The food consisted of yummy sandwiches, chicken bites, sausage rolls, crisps, prawn vol-au-vents and iced biscuits. Millie's mother had baked a super birthday cake in the shape of an eight to show how old Millie was. The children played a variety of games like 'Musical

Statues' and were just going to play 'Pass the Parcel' when Mrs. Mason exclaimed.

'Where is Josie? Can someone find her or she will miss out on all the fun!'

Pinky offered to look for Josie while the children sat themselves into a large ring. Pinky could not find Josie anywhere downstairs so she began to look in the bedrooms. Pinky opened the door to Mr. and Mrs. Mason's bedroom and there was Josie opening wardrobe doors and drawers. She had pulled out a heap of Mrs. Mason's jewellery and had begun to try on necklaces and bracelets. She had dressed herself in one of Mrs. Mason's dresses and had put a bright red feather boa around her neck. A pair of high heels flopped around on Josie's feet.

Well! Thought Pinky. This little girl is not so much of a Josie Parker as a Nosy Parker!!

'Josie!' exclaimed Pinky. 'What are you doing? Please put all these things away and come downstairs at once. Everyone is waiting for you so that they can start playing 'Pass the Parcel'.'

'Oh,' replied Josie in an offhand way. 'I just want to try on a few more pairs of shoes and then I'll come down.'

Pinky stared at her in astonishment. What a cheeky little girl! How dare she touch someone's belongings without asking, thought Pinky.

Pinky said no more and went downstairs. She thought Josie was very naughty! Pinky had spent a lifetime of curing children of their naughty habits and she decided to do something to stop Josie behaving so badly.

While everybody sat chatting, waiting for Josie, Pinky went to her bag which she had left in the hall and took out a glass tube of luminous magic liquid. She took a Shocking Choccy Woc out of her bag and covered the sweet with the magic liquid. Then fetching a big, glass dish from the kitchen, Pinky made an arrangement of the sweets she had brought with her and right on the top of the sweets, she placed the Shocking Choccy Woc.

By now, Josie had come downstairs and was dressed once again in her own clothes. While the children played 'Pass the Parcel', Pinky took around the dish of sweets which she offered first to Josie. The Shocking Choccy Woc which Pinky had coated with magic dust was glowing brightly and attracted to it, Josie took it off the top of the sweets and popped it into her mouth.

'Mmm, delicious! You do make such tasty sweets Mrs. Spinks,' commented Josie. By now, the other children had chosen their sweets and there were popping sounds and fizzing sounds all around.

'Coo,' said one little boy. 'My sweet just went poof in my mouth and it's gone now, so can I have another please?'

It didn't take long before all the sweets were eaten. The 'Pass the Parcel' games were the last games to be played and soon the mothers and fathers came to collect their children.

Josie went into the kitchen to get a drink while her mother waited with Mrs. Mason.

Suddenly, there was a cry from outside the door of the room where the two mothers were sitting.

Amazingly, A LONG NOSE WAS WRIGGLING AROUND THE DOOR!!

It poked into the sideboard where it began to crash and bash about as though it was looking for something.

Mrs. Parker and Mrs. Mason were stunned to see it!

'What is it?' cried Mrs Mason, screaming as she jumped up onto one of the chairs. ' What is that monstrous thing?'

'I've no idea!' replied Mrs. Parker as she stood in

the farthest corner of the room. 'But, I don't like the look of it, really I don't!'

'It looks like a long wriggly snake!' cried Mrs. Mason. 'Surely, it can't be a snake! Where would it have come from?'

Just then, Josie came into the room, trying to hold up her nose. Although it was very spongy it was still heavy to carry!

'Josie!' gasped Mrs. Parker. 'Have you been up to your old tricks again, sticking your nose into matters that don't concern you?'

Shame-faced, Josie sat on the floor and could not look her mother in the eye.

'Well, I can't believe it!' exclaimed Mrs. Mason as she climbed down off her chair. 'Is it really Josie's nose? What are we going to do? Josie can't go home with her nose trailing along the ground, can she?'

'No. she can't,' said Mrs. Parker firmly. 'But I have an idea. Have you any ribbon Mrs. Mason? I was thinking we could tie it up!'

AND, that is exactly what the two mothers did. Between them, they gathered up the nose, tying the ends of the ribbon around Josie's ears.

'Oh dear!' exclaimed Mrs. Parker. 'What a sight you look Josie. Thank goodness all the other children have gone home. Luckily, it's getting dark now and when we get home I'll ring the doctor and get you an appointment in the morning as early as I can. But, I don't know if the doctor will be able to shrink it. I've never seen anything like it. It's extraordinary! Well! I dare say you deserve it. Really! You must stop poking your nose into things!'

Poor Josie and her mother walked home slowly. The nose made Josie's face ache so that when she got home, she wanted to go to bed.

'Yes, I think you should. I don't know what Daddy will say when he sees it,' commented Mrs Parker, for now she was quite agitated about it.

Josie went to bed while Mrs. Parker telephoned the doctor to make an appointment for the next morning. But, did Josie go to the doctor the next morning? NO, SHE DIDN'T! Pinky had coated the sweet Josie had eaten with the magic liquid very lightly, so that by the morning the magic had worn off.

But, it was a lesson learned! Yes, definitely a lesson learned. Josie was so pleased her nose was back to its normal size that from then on there was a distinct improvement in her behaviour. And, it was all down to Mrs. Pinky Spinks magic!!

THE CAT CAT-ASTROPHE

CHAPTER FOUR

Early one morning, just before opening time, Pinky went into the shop and sniffed and sniffed. What was that awful smell? She looked around her carefully. Was the smell coming from the Fishy Fudge Fricasees? Yes, it was! 'Oh no!' exclaimed Pinky out loud. 'Perhaps the fish powder was too strong!'

She took the Fishy Fudge Fricasees out of the window. On the other hand, she wondered, it's rather warm today, perhaps they've just gone off!

She put the Fricasees into the bin in the kitchen, then went into the storeroom to get some ingredients to make some more. She reached up to a shelf on the dresser in the kitchen where she had put some magic powders.

Suddenly, Sidney shot through the cat flap into the kitchen, chased by a big black and white cat. Sidney was very scared and jumped up onto the dresser. He flicked his tail to and fro angrily and knocked half a dozen boxes of magic powders off the shelf.

'Oh, goodness, gracious me!' exclaimed Pinky. She shooed the black and white cat out of the kitchen and went to get a spoon to scoop up the magic powders. She thought she had scooped up most of the powders and put them back into the right boxes.

BUT DID SHE?

Pinky proceeded to make some more Fishy Fudge Fricasees. Once she had made the mixture (she never told ANYONE about her secret recipes), she poured the mixture into two big sweet tins and popped them in the oven.

Pinky went into her sitting room and while she waited for the Fricasees to bake, she read her favourite magazine called 'Magic For Magicians and Wizards.'

Suddenly, BOOM!! BOOM!! BOOM!! Startled, Pinky jumped up out of her armchair and rushed into the kitchen. The Fricasees had risen in the tins so much that there wasn't enough room for them in the oven and the oven door had blown off!!

There was now a strong smell of baked fish coming from the oven and the Fricasee mixture began to pour out of the oven and on to the floor.

All at once, cats came jumping through the cat flap and soon the kitchen was filling up with cats. Marmalade coloured cats, black cats, tabby cats, tortoiseshell cats, white cats, fluffy cats and scruffy cats! THE KITCHEN WAS FULL OF CATS. BIG ONES, SMALL ONES AND ALL SORTS! They began to lick up the Fricasee mixture off the floor as it had spread everywhere!

'Oh goodness!' groaned Pinky. 'Some of the magic powder must have got mixed up and made the Fricasees rise up too much!' How was she going to clear up the sticky mess? But, she didn't have to worry! Oh no! The cats were ecstatic about the unusual tasty treat and licked it all up from the floor.

Pinky tried to push the cats, one by one, out of the cat flap but they were too fat! She opened the kitchen door and shooed them out of the door with her broom. Fortunately, they didn't want to hang around anyway. Since there was no more mixture left to eat!

The fat cats waddled up Pinky's garden path and gradually, after sitting in the sun and washing their whiskers, they disappeared in ones and twos.

Feeling very flustered, Pinky sank down into her armchair to think what she should do next. First thing was to clean the still sticky floor and then telephone Mr. Tibbs the odd job man to fix her oven door back into place.

'Well!' exclaimed Pinky after Mr. Tibbs had left. 'In future I will stick to making Funky Fudge Bites. In any case they are more popular than the Fishy Fudge Fricasees.'

As for Sidney, outnumbered by all the cats, he had fled upstairs to Pinky's bedroom and didn't appear again until teatime.

HAIRY TAILS

CHAPTER FIVE

    A couple of days passed after Pinky's cat cat-
astrophe without anything more eventful occurring.
Then, on Wednesday morning, Pinky heard Sidney
scratching at the kitchen door and mewing mournfully.

'Miaow, MIAOW, MIAOW, MIAOW!'

Pinky opened the door and in stalked Sidney, a very upset Sidney, waving his tail pitifully in the air, he turned to show Pinky what was wrong with him.

'Oh goodness me!' exclaimed Pinky. 'What has happened to your beautiful, furry tail?'

Poor Sidney's tail had lost the hair on the end of it and the skin there was a deep, pinky red and blistering.

'Dear, oh dear,' gasped Pinky. 'How did your tail get in such a state? I must ring the vet to get an appointment for you at once!'

Pinky was very lucky and there was a spare appointment available at 11.00 a.m. She turned the sign on the shop door from 'open' to 'closed'. Then, she put Sidney into his cat basket very carefully and hurried to the bus stop to catch the next bus into town. Poor Sidney mewed all the way so that the other people on the bus kept asking what was wrong with him.

'I'm not sure,' said Pinky, shaking her head sadly. 'However, I'm sure the vet will be able to tell me and make him better.'

When the vet examined Sidney, he was shocked at what he saw. 'I think,' he remarked, shaking his head angrily, 'someone has tied a firework, probably a banger to Sidney's tail. Who would be so cruel? Has anyone near you had a party recently and let off fireworks to celebrate?'

'No, I don't think so,' replied Pinky. 'And yet, now I

come to think about it, there were some bangs and whizzes coming from somewhere behind my house last night.'

'Mm,' said the vet. 'If I were you I would keep Sidney in for a few days to make sure nothing else happens to him. Meanwhile, I'll give you some cream for his tail which you must rub in twice a day.'

A very sad Pinky caught the next bus home and pondered the matter. She knew most of the children and grown-ups in the village and couldn't believe any of them would be so cruel to harm her cat like that.

After lunch, Pinky opened her shop again to see two children waiting outside.

'Hello,' said Pinky. 'I don't believe I have seen you before, or have I? I'm getting old now and my memory is not so good.'

'No,' replied a girl. My brother and I have just moved here and we don't start school until tomorrow. We live a couple of streets away. We had a super-duper welcome party last night for all our family to celebrate our moving to our new home.'

'Yes,' enthused her brother. 'It was fab! We had lots of fireworks too!'

At the word fireworks Pinky's ears pricked up. Suddenly, Sidney stalked into the shop from the kitchen where he had been feeling lonely. He began to rub his sides against Pinky's legs.

'Heh, Debbie. Isn't that the cat that we... you know!' said Harry as he winked at his sister.

'Yeah, Harry it is but ssh, don't say any more.' replied Debbie as she nudged her brother.

Oh! thought Pinky. So you two are the ones that have been so cruel to my cat. I should report you to the police! But, oh dear, I can't prove it was you. Still, I have got a way to show you how nasty you have been.

Debbie and Harry bought some Rainbow Rockets and Liquory Lick Licks and left the shop. Hastily, Pinky turned the shop sign to 'closed' again and hurried after them.   She fairly scampered along as she tried to keep up with them as they headed for the play area on the village green.

Pinky went over to talk to one of her neighbours, Chrissie Underwood, who was pushing her toddler on a baby swing. At the same time she saw Debbie and Harry go on the slide, roundabout and see-saw. She knew soon they would go on the swings so she edged over to the swings and sprinkled some crushed Pumfy Pom Poms onto the two swings. Pumfy Pom Poms were her strongest magic and as she sprinkled the dusty bits onto the two swings she said loudly, 'Hairy Tails! Hairy Tails!'

Debbie and Harry were laughing together as they went up and down on the see-saw. 'Come on, Harry,' shouted Debbie. 'We haven't been on the swings yet!' Both children ran to the swings and began to work them to and fro. 'Higher, higher,' called out Harry. 'Look I'm much higher than you Debbie, you're as slow as a snail!'

Meanwhile, Pinky had gone back to Chrissie to tell her about the sweet stall she was going to open at the forthcoming market on Saturday.

'I think that's a jolly good idea, you having a sweet stall at the market.' commented Chrissie. 'Everyone loves your scrumptious sweets Pinky and it will give people from the other villages a chance to buy them. But make sure you have enough left for us. I don't know what we would do now without your amazing sweets.'

Chrissie decided it was time for her to go home and waving goodbye to Pinky, she set off. Just then Debbie and Harry decided to go home too and got off the swings.

'Heh! Harry!' remarked Debbie. 'There's a funny, bumpy thing coming out of your jeans at the back. Oh wow! It's a tail, a long, long tail.' Debbie could not stop laughing.

'You do look funny, Harry. Your tail is waving to and fro like a pendulum on a clock!'

Suddenly, Debbie's own bottom began to itch and when she felt around her back she had a tail too. She screamed.' What's happening to us?' she cried. 'Oh, what is happening? We can't go to school tomorrow like this!'

Harry's tail was black and white striped like a zebra's while Debbie's tail was brown and cream striped and matched her dress perfectly. Pinky was always spot on with her magic!!

Now that she could see her magic had worked, Pinky decided to go home. She went across the green to speak to Debbie and Harry.

'Hello,' she said. 'Didn't you just come into my shop and buy some sweets?'

'Yes,' replied Debbie. ' But oh, Mrs. Spinks look! We've grown tails. What are we to do? Mum and Dad will be so angry with us. They will think we have been naughty again. AND they are cats' tails. We hate cats don't we Harry?'

'Well,' replied Pinky. 'Have you been unkind to any cat lately? It seems to me that someone is punishing you for something you shouldn't have done.'

Harry and Debbie went bright red in the face.

'Can you help us, Mrs Spinks?' asked Harry. 'We can't go home like this!'

'You can come home with me,' replied Pinky, beginning to feel a little sorry for them. 'You can help me in the garden which will keep you busy. I will phone your parents and say you are stopping for a sleep-over.' For, Pinky knew the magic would wear off by the morning and the two children would be back to normal.

Debbie and Harry carried their tails under their coats and woefully followed Pinky home. They did some work in Pinky's garden and Pinky gave them some tea. She gave them sardines on toast and some milk to drink. Sardines were Sidney's favourite food! Perhaps they will realise how lucky they are as children to eat my scrumptious sweets, thought Pinky. Cats aren't allowed to eat sweets and have a dreadfully boring diet!

Before they went to bed, Harry and Debbie saw Sidney curled up in his basket by the fire. Debbie began to stroke him.

'You know, Mrs Spinks,' she declared. 'Cats are quite nice really, aren't they?' But Sidney was having none of it! He remembered who had tied the firework to his tail and indignantly stalked out of the room. Going upstairs, he curled up on Pinky's bed instead and went to sleep.

'I don't think Sidney likes you very much!' commented Pinky. 'I wonder why that is?'

Debbie looked at Harry in a very guilty fashion. Quickly, she changed the subject of the conversation.

'Can we go to bed now?' she asked Pinky. 'All that gardening has made me tired.'

Both children took it in turns to go into Pinky's bathroom and they did wash and brush each other's tails before they went to bed!!

'Please, oh please, let our tails be gone by tomorrow morning,' moaned Debbie.

'Yeah,' replied Harry. 'Actually, I do think your tail looks a bit shorter. But I'll never be cruel to animals again, Debbie. I think Mrs. Spinks is right. Someone is punishing us. Heh! You don't think it was Mrs. Spinks do you?

'Oh no!' answered Debbie. 'She's such a nice old lady. I'M SURE SHE WOULDN'T DO SUCH A THING!'

CHAPTER SIX

On Saturday morning, Pinky woke up early as she was so excited about the opening of her sweet stall at the open-air market. She packed four large pink and white candy striped bags with lots of her sweets. She made sure she put in plenty of Liquory Lick Licks, Rainbow Rockets, Melting Mallows, Sherbert Sizzlers, Shocking Choccy Wocs and Grinning Gobstoppers as they seemed to be amongst the most popular sweets. Max and Oliver were going to help her set up the stall and then they would serve the customers for Pinky. Pinky really liked Max and Oliver as they were very kind boys and often did little jobs for her. They belonged to a boys club and had earned lots of badges in a whole range of activities.

Pinky put a notice on the door which said,' Closed Until Lunchtime.' It was now 8.00 a.m. and when she opened the shop door there stood Max and Oliver looking eager and excited.

'Please, Mrs. Spinks,' said Oliver. 'We're here to help you with the new sweet stall.'

'Yes!' Max nodded his head in agreement. 'I just can't wait to set it up. All those lovely sweets to sell to our friends, they'll be so envious!'

'Yes, but just make sure you don't eat too many!'

Pinky said tartly. She noticed that both boys had on pink hooded tops with the words 'Spinks Sweets' printed on the front. She had them made up especially and thought they would make a good impression on the would-be buyers!

By the time they reached the open-air market some stall holders had already set up their goods on their stalls There were homemade loaves of bread and cakes for sale, fresh fruit and vegetables from local farms, fresh fish and meats. Other stalls were selling toys, games, pots and pans, handbags, jewellery and sports equipment.

Max and Oliver went to the village hall and brought back a large folding table which they set up between them. Pinky covered the table with a big plastic cloth with yes, you've guessed it! Pink roses all over it since pink roses were her favourite flowers! Pinky put all the sweets in different sized bags at the back of the table and bowls of the same sweets at the front of the stall so people could see what they were buying.

By now, most of the village people had arrived carrying their shopping bags. Also, there were a lot of people Pinky didn't know and she guessed they came from the nearby town and other villages. The village green looked as though it was covered with brightly coloured butterflies as people fluttered to and fro to look at the different stalls.

Just as Pinky was about to return to her shop, a van with Potts's Puppies painted on the side of it, parked in the road behind Pinky's stall which was close to the pavement. A mean looking man got out of the van and opened the back doors. He began to bring out wire cages, each with a puppy in it. He stacked the cages one on top of the other until they formed tiers of three. The price of each puppy was pinned to a card on each cage.

Pinky looked at the cages very carefully. She became very angry as she saw that some of the bigger puppies didn't have room to stand up or turn around. In fact, all the cages were too small and none contained any water for the puppies to drink. Although it was only March it was a warm, sunny day. Some of the puppies were whimpering whilst others stared forlornly out of their cages.

Goodness me! thought Pinky. I don't think I like this Mr. Potts very much. Those poor puppies! If this is how they are treated when they are on show, how are they treated at Mr. Potts's house? In fact, unknown to Pinky, Mr. Potts kept the puppies in a cold, draughty barn where they had no contact with the outside world until they were put into the tiny cages and hauled around different markets.

Pinky hurried back to her shop to see what she could find to sort out what was a very big problem. She had to save those poor puppies from their miserable lives! She hurried into her workroom to see what she had in the way of 'Vanishing Powder.' She collected up lots of bottles and mixed the contents up. After all the

'Vanishing Powder' had to be very strong to work on all those cages. She put the powders into a big pot and made a lot of holes in the lid.

Pinky returned to the market and said 'Hello!' to Mr. Potts. Then, pretending she wanted to buy a puppy, she walked past all the puppy cages shaking the 'Vanishing Powder' over them until they were well coated with the magic dust.

Suddenly, the wire cages began to melt! Each puppy just sat there unaware that they were free. Then, as though connected by the same thought, they scrambled up. Their paws hardly touching the ground, they frolicked around the green like new-born lambs, yapping and yelping with puppy glee. Eventually, a big puppy began to head in the direction of the woods and the others soon followed it!

Mr. Potts was frantic! 'Help! Help! Someone help me! My puppies have all escaped!' He shouted out.' Help me catch my puppies! Help me catch those doggy rascals!' But, not one person offered to help Mr. Potts. Other people had noticed how tightly the puppies had been crammed into their cages. They were pleased the puppies had escaped!

Mr. Potts spent most of the morning searching for the puppies but by 1.00 o'clock when it was time for the market to close, he gave up reluctantly. Despondently, he drove his van away, vowing to himself that he would search the woods later in the hope of finding the puppies.

Somehow, he could not have had any luck! For after teatime, when it started to get dark, each house and cottage in the village heard whimpering and scratching outside their front doors. Doors were opened and squeals of delight could be heard. Puppies were gathered up and given some very strange names like Fizz, Zizzi, Cracker, Fudge and Midget!

As for Mr. Potts? He hadn't a phone number in the phone directory. People in the village enquired of him in the nearby town and in the surrounding villages for they felt they should pay for their puppies. However, no'one knew where he had come from!

As for Pinky? She had made a lot of money from her sweet stall. It would be Easter soon and she wanted to put the money towards making a special Easter Egg into which she would put a magic wish. But, THAT'S ANOTHER STORY!

ROSIE BOTTOM

CHAPTER SEVEN

Rosie Bottom lived in a big house overlooking the village green. She had no brothers or sisters and as a result she was terribly spoilt. She was very bossy and liked to be the first to do anything. If that meant pushing other children out of the way, she pushed them with her bottom.

'Rosie!' exclaimed her mother one day when she was watching Rosie playing in the garden with her friends.

'You might be Bottom by name but you needn't use your bottom to push everyone out of the way!'

Rosie's mother sighed as she watched Rosie push one little girl off her bicycle. Rosie had the bike for her birthday and she didn't want anyone else to ride it. Rosie sat her own bottom firmly on the bicycle instead.

'Whee! Look at me! Look at me!' shouted Rosie as she whizzed around the garden.

'You two can't ride a bike as well as me!'

'We don't get a chance!' retorted Ellie. 'Since you always have to be first to go on anything!'

Ellie was the little girl that Rosie had pushed off the bicycle and she went into the house to ask if she could go home.

'Please Mrs. Bottom. Can you phone my Mum and ask her to come and collect me?' she asked 'I don't want to play with Rosie anymore, she's too rough.'

'Of course Ellie. I'll phone your mother right now.' replied Mrs. Bottom.

Very soon, the other little girl, Gemma was pushed over by Rosie because Rosie had wanted to be first to go on the trampoline. Gemma began to cry as she had grazed her knee badly.

Mrs. Bottom called Gemma into the kitchen and put a plaster on her knee.

'There!' she exclaimed 'That should keep your knee clean and stop it bleeding. I'll phone your mother and ask her to fetch you.'

After Mrs. Bottom had made the tea, Rosie did her homework and went up to her bedroom to finish reading a book she had started reading the day before.

Mr. and Mrs. Bottom sat and talked about what could be done to stop Rosie from being so selfish. They could not think of anything that would cure Rosie.

'You know what,' said Mrs. Bottom to her husband. 'Tomorrow, I think I'll ask Mrs. Spinks if she could give me any advice. She is a very wise, old lady and might be able to tell us how to cure Rosie. If Rosie goes on pushing other children she won't have any friends left!'

The next morning, Mrs. Bottom took Rosie to school and stopped at Mrs. Spinks shop on her way home.

Pinky was busy building some boxes of Squidgy Squiggles into a big pyramid in the middle of her shop window.

'What can I do for you, Mrs. Bottom?' asked Pinky. 'Do you want to buy some of these delicious Squidgy Squiggles? I can definitely recommend them. They are my latest creation.'

Mrs. Bottom shook her head and tearfully told Pinky about Rosie's behaviour.

Pinky looked very thoughtful. 'What is Rosie going to be doing after school today?' she asked Mrs. Bottom. 'I do think I have a cure for Rosie's behaviour but you mus'n't interfere with my methods. Is that agreed?'

Mrs. Bottom nodded her head. 'Anything, do

anything you wish Mrs. Spinks. I am desperate!
Nothing I have tried so far has made any difference
to Rosie's behaviour. She is going to the playground
after school and I have arranged to pick her up from
there at 5.00 o'clock.'

'Right you are!' commented Pinky. 'I'll meet you
then.'

At four o'clock, Pinky went to the playground and
saw Rosie push another child out of the way so that
she could be first to go down the slide.

Pinky went to the roundabout which had several,
separate seats on it. Pinky stuck some Puff Up
Pastilles in the four corners of one of the seats. Then
she called out to Rosie.

'There's nobody on this roundabout Rosie! Why
don't you be first to go on it. I'll give you a push and
you can see how fast you can go!'

Rosie came running over to the roundabout, calling to
her friends to join her.

'Wow! Thanks Mrs. Spinks,' she said, smiling. 'That
is really kind of you to let me go on first.' She had no
idea about what would happen next!!

Pinky watched Rosie scramble onto the seat she had
stuck the Puff Up Pastilles on and once Gemma and
Ellie had climbed on, Pinky began to push the
roundabout quickly.

After a few minutes, as they whizzed by, everyone
could hear, brrp, brrp, brrp, pa-a-arp!!' Then, one more
PARP!!

'Rosie!' exclaimed Gemma. 'You're blowing windy woos! I can hear them! They are really loud. That's really rude!'

Rosie went red in the face. 'Can you stop the roundabout, Mrs. Spinks?' she called. 'I can't move my bottom in this seat. It seems to be stuck!'

'Brrp, brrp, brrp, parp PARP! PARP! went Rosie's bottom which was getting squeezed even more in her seat. Her bottom had swelled to twice its normal size! Brrp, brrp, parp, PARP!!

'Oh, I can't get out of this seat!' cried Rosie. 'I'm stuck fast. What's happening to my bottom? It's enormous! Please Mrs. Spinks, can you help me?'

'It's no good Rosie!' exclaimed Pinky. 'In fact, I think your bottom is still growing. There's no way I can ease you out of your seat. You'll just have to stay there until it goes back to its normal size.'

'But that could take simply ages!' cried Rosie.

Meanwhile, Rosie's BRPS and PARPS could be heard all over the playground. Some of the children intrigued by the PARPS had come over to the roundabout to see what was making the funny noises.

'Why is this happening to me?' cried Rosie. Then, pointing to Gemma and Ellie she said. 'Look! They are okay aren't they?'

'Honestly Rosie', replied Gemma. 'If only you didn't keep pushing other people out of the way to get what you want, this probably would not have happened! I think someone is punishing you and you jolly well deserve it!'

'Oh, I'm sorry!' cried Rosie. 'I know I'm selfish. I really will try to share things more fairly in future. Really I will.'

The minute Rosie apologised for her bad behaviour her bottom began to shrink. Only a tiny bit, but it was a start!

By now, Mr and Mrs. Bottom had arrived. Mrs. Bottom looked at Pinky and winked at her.

'Is everything all right here, Mrs Spinks?' asked Mrs. Bottom. 'I've come to take Rosie home. But it looks like Rosie is stuck in her seat. Goodness me! Look at the size of her bottom. How did it get so big?'

Edging towards Rosie's seat, Pinky managed to pull off the Puff Up Pastilles without Rosie seeing her.

'Oh, it's okay Mum.' Said Rosie. 'I think I might be able to wriggle out of this seat now, but I'll need a bit of help.'

After a lot of pushing this way and that way, Rosie was pulled out of her seat with a loud POP! POP! POP!

With all the excitement over, gradually everyone went home for their tea. ONLY Rosie walked home rubbing her sore bottom in the hope it would shrink a bit more. Pinky's magic had triumphed again.

The Huge, Hairy, Hound-Dog

Chapter Eight

One day in the week, halfway through the morning, Pinky went into her kitchen to make a cup of tea. She took it with her back into the shop. As she looked around at her sweet displays, she noticed that a large number of Peanut Patties and Fishy Fudge Fricasees were missing from one of the lower shelves. How strange, she thought. I'm sure that they were there when the last customers went out.

She sat down behind the counter to drink her tea and read the local newspaper. On the front of the newspaper were the headlines, 'Sausages and Pies Go Missing Again' The butcher had pies and sausages go missing from his counter. The baker had some sausage rolls taken. The grocer had apples and bananas missing from his stall.

'Well!' Pinky exclaimed aloud. 'Now, I've lost some of my sweets. Who can the culprit be?'

Just then, the shop bell tinkled as two children came into the shop leaving the door open. Pinky turned around to reach for the Happy Humbugs that were on a high shelf behind her. (she wasn't getting many requests these days for Happy Humbugs as the children seemed to be really happy eating all the other sweets) The children paid for the sweets and then went out closing the door behind them.

After they had left the shop, Pinky noticed that some more sweets were missing. 'Goodness, gracious me!' exclaimed Pinky. 'At this rate I won't have enough sweets to sell.'

Then, Pinky had a good idea. Next time the shop doorbell went she would hide behind the counter and watch.

It wasn't long before a little girl came in, once again leaving the door open. Pinky was just about to fully show herself when peeping over the counter, she saw a huge, hairy dog rush in behind the little girl, snap up some Choccy Wocs in its powerful jaws and bound out of the shop again. The little girl hadn't even seen it come and go!

Pinky served the little girl, then turned the 'open sign' on the shop door to 'closed'. Quite shaken, after all it had been a very big hairy dog, she sat down to think about what she had seen. Pinky liked animals and wondered why the dog was so hungry that it was forced to steal food. Perhaps it wasn't being fed properly! After all, a dog that size would need to eat a lot. She decided she would go out, walk around carefully and see if the dog was still around.

Suddenly, 'yes, there it is!' exclaimed Pinky as she watched the dog snatch some sausages from the butcher's front stall. The dog now seemed to be in no hurry, content to know it had plenty of sausages, it trotted along towards the direction of the woods.

Pinky followed it at a distance, not taking her eyes off the dog as it carried the sausages which were swinging from side to side. Eventually, they reached the woods and the dog bounded into a clearing which was ringed by big bushes. Suddenly, the dog darted under a bush. Pinky decided she would pluck up the courage to look under the bush! If the dog had a collar on it, it might have the name and phone number on it and then she could contact the owner and ask the owner to collect it.

'Wow!' Pinky was shocked to her pinky toes! There lay the dog with eight little puppies curled against it. There were banana skins, paper wrappings and other debris from the stolen food strewn around. Although the dog was huge, Pinky was not afraid of it. The dog gazed woefully at Pinky and thumped its tail hopefully on the ground.

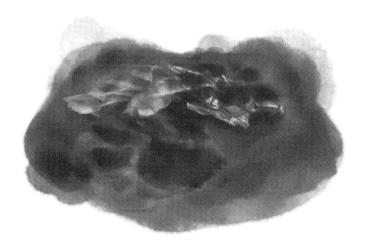

'You poor thing!' exclaimed Pinky. 'No wonder you have been stealing food with all these puppies to feed. You should be eating proper dog food too, not sweets and bananas. You don't have a collar either do you so you must be a stray. Such a pity!'

Pinky stood there staring at the dog wondering what she should do. If she went home and phoned the 'Home For Unwanted Dogs', it might stay in the home for months. It was such a big dog she doubted it would find a home quickly. Why, with one sweep of its powerful tail it could easily knock things over and break them!!

Then, she had a FANTASTIC idea. She could hear Mr. Brown's tractor going up and down in the field next to the woods. Climbing over a style and into the field, Pinky rushed towards the tractor waving her arms. The tractor stopped and Farmer Brown climbed down from it.

'What's the matter, Pinky?' He asked. 'What is so important that you have to interrupt my ploughing. My, if you don't look as pink as your name!'

Pinky was huffing and puffing but asked Farmer Brown if he could go back to his farm and bring back Bessie his horse and the farm cart.

'Whatever for Pinky?' he asked.

'I have found a huge dog in the woods. I don't know what breed it is but it has eight puppies with it. It's a stray and has been stealing food from the village shops! If you could bring your cart we can collect them and then decide what to do with them. They can't stay out in the woods where they will get wet when it rains and also with the nights being cold at the moment!'

Farmer Brown took off his cap and scratched his head.

'Well now,' he remarked. 'I think I had better come and see this dog first. I don't want to pick it up and try and put it in the cart in case it bites me!'

'I don't think it will.' replied Pinky. 'It is a huge dog but I think it is sad and lonely. It just needs a good home and room for its puppies.'

Farmer Brown went back to his farm and came back driving his horse and cart. Pinky led the way and when they got to where the dog and its puppies were Farmer Brown got down from his cart and looked at the dog thoughtfully.

'You know what, Pinky!' he exclaimed. 'I'll keep it. I've been looking for a guard dog for the farm. This dog is so big it would scare anyone away who might think about stealing my tractor!'

Just then the dog barked, but it was wagging its enormous tail and looking at Farmer Brown quizzically as if to say, 'Yes, I am a big dog but please help me!'

'See what I mean Pinky! That bark is really scary isn't it? I think she and I will get on really well.'

Pinky helped put the dog and its puppies into the cart and they all went back to the farm. Farmer Brown took the dog and its puppies into a nice warm barn and made them up a cosy bed away from any draughts. Then, he gave them something to eat and drink.

Farmer Brown invited Pinky into the farm kitchen where they had some tea with freshly baked scones, cream and strawberry jam. Afterwards, Farmer Brown took Pinky home, promising to let her know how the dog and her puppies got on.

Farmer Brown was delighted with the dog which he named K2 after the second largest mountain in the world! When the puppies were older, he found them homes with some of his farmer friends. It was clear the puppies would be big dogs one day just like their mother.

AND a news reporter came to Pinky's shop to ask her how she had solved the mystery of the missing food and found the huge, hairy dog a home. The very next morning there was a picture of Pinky, Farmer Brown, and K2 on the front page of the local newspaper! Pinky was famous!!

On this occasion, Pinky had not had to use any magic to make things right. But she didn't mind, oh no she didn't! She had found the huge, hairy hound-dog AND by way of her actions, all the puppies new homes. What more could she ask for? Just a sit down by the fire in a cosy corner of her cottage with a nice cup of tea and a sticky bun!!

THE EXTRAORDINARY, EGNORMOUS EASTER EGG

CHAPTER NINE

It was the week before Easter and there was to be a fete on the village green on Saturday next. The village church roof needed some repairs and all the proceeds of the fete would go to paying for the repairs.

Pinky had decided that she would make a very big Easter Egg and charge people 5 pence a go to guess how much it weighed. Not only that, it was to be a magic egg for whoever guessed the weight correctly would have the egg and a magic wish which she would put inside. Not that Pinky knew how to make a magic wish but she knew there were some books on magic in her loft that used to belong to her father.

She fetched a ladder and climbed into the loft and began to search around. Finally, behind a very big cobweb with a very fat spider sitting in it, she found a huge box of books. She began looking through the books, putting aside books like 'Naughty Wizardry for Nutty People' until she found a book entitled, 'The Bonkers Book of Magic Making.' Just the job, she thought to herself, this looks like it's what I need.

Hastily, she climbed down the ladder and took the book to the kitchen. She brushed off the dust on the cover and flicked through the pages until she came to a page that said, 'How to Make a First Rate Magic Wish.'

'Coo, just the thing,' remarked Pinky excitedly. 'After all I don't want a second-rate magic wish do I?' She began to read out all the magic ingredients and went to fetch them from her store room. She weighed them carefully and put them into a large mixing bowl.

'Well, here I go,' she said out loud. 'I hope I can say the magic words properly.' She conjured up a deep, mysterious voice and began to recite,

'Wiggle, wiggle winky wham,
Mix them up in the magic pan,
Throw in truffles, tincture, tumbs,
Then some crinkly, crunchy crumbs.
Stir them up in the magic dish,
Shazam! Shazam! A magic wish!'

After Pinky had uttered all the magic words, she read a sentence underneath which said 'Roll the wish in some bubble gum and keep it in a cool place.'

Pinky was very excited. She had succeeded in making her first magic wish! She did as she was instructed and put the wish in some bubble gum, then into a fancy wrapper and then she twisted both ends of the paper so that the wish could not fall out. Now all she had to do was make the Easter Egg!

On Sunday morning Pinky began to make the

chocolate egg. Not only did she have to mix up a lot of chocolate but she had to make a big box to put it in.

First, she made two cardboard egg-shaped castes into which she poured the chocolate mix. When the chocolate had set hard, she took the two halves out of the castes. Into one half, she put the magic wish. In the other half of the chocolate egg, she added a mix of small sweets, Candy Cats, Mini Mallows and Tinky Tots. Then, she stuck the two chocolate halves together, sealing them with Juicy Jello. Finally, she wrapped the egg in some brightly coloured wrapping paper. She looked at the chocolate egg in delight. It was a superlicious, so delicious, yummy, scrummy Easter Egg!!

The next Saturday, Pinky went to the village hall and picked out the biggest folding table she could find. With the help of other stall holders, she hoisted the Extraordinary, Egnormous Easter Egg onto the table and put a cardboard notice next to it which said 'Guess the weight of this extra special chocolate Easter egg. Only 5p a go, the egg also contains a magic wish for the winner!'

It wasn't long before children of all ages and sizes came to look at THE EGG. They were entranced! ' Look Mum,' said one little boy. 'Only five pence to guess the weight AND it would last me for a whole year if we put it in the fridge. So, you wouldn't have to buy me any more sweets.'

   'Well, that's a fact,' replied his mother as she eagerly offered twenty pence for four guesses.
   People were all around the stall. Clamouring to offer their money to try to win the magic Easter Egg. In fact, Pinky was kept busy all day long! By four o'clock, all her sweets were sold and her money-box was full of five pence pieces. Pinky took the box of money and the list of peoples' names and their guesses to Mrs. Sproggins, the fete organiser. Almost immediately, Mrs. Sproggins called through her megaphone that it was time to announce the prize winners. Pinky's 'Guess the weight of the Easter Egg' was the last to be announced.
   'And the winner of the Extraordinary, Egnormous Easter Egg is.... ', as Mrs. Sproggins hesitated, all the

children sitting around the green held their breath.
'It's Tanny Tibbs who guessed the correct weight of
10 lb and 7 ounces.'

'Cor luv a duck!' shouted Mrs. Tibbs. 'Tanny, you've
won!'

Tanny's brother Tommy rushed home to get a
wheelbarrow to push the chocolate egg in and all the
Tibbs family helped to get the chocolate egg into it.
Proudly, Tanny began to push the chocolate egg home.
Some other children came up to Tanny as she carefully
pushed the egg which was wobbling a bit from side to
side.

'What are you going to wish for, Tanny?' asked one of
her friends.

'Ooh, I don't think I should tell anyone in case it
doesn't come true. But once I've made the wish and it
does come true, I'll tell you what it was!'

All the children went home feeling a bit envious.
Would Tanny wish for a big house for their big family
to live in? Or, maybe a super swanky car?

When Mrs. Tibbs and her family reached home,
Tanny could see her wish had come true. For there
standing on the doorstep was Mr. Tibbs out of hospital
at last! Tanny had wished he would get well enough to
come home.

'My wish has come true, yippee!' shouted Tanny as
she raced up the path to their cottage. 'Oh, thank you
Mrs. Spinks. You are the bestest magicking lady I have
ever met!'

ERNIE'S EARS

CHAPTER TEN

Ernie's full name was Ernest. His mother's name was Hope and his father was named Christian. It was a tradition in their family to have names that said something about them as people. Ernie was certainly Ernest by nature because he couldn't help listening to other peoples' private conversations EARNESTLY and telling everyone what he heard.

One Saturday, Ernie was standing in a queue in Pinky's shop behind two little girls, named Emily and Sarah. His ears were twitching as he listened to what they were saying. In no time at all, he had learned that Emily couldn't do her sums and that Sarah was still reading 'a first reader' instead of being up to level 3 where most of the other children had got to.

On the following Monday morning, just before break, Ernie's class had been learning about the volcanoes and mountains of the world. Now, Ernie was clever at doing sums and reading but he had a bad memory when trying to remember the names of important people and places. Emily and Sarah were delighted with their scores in the Geography test whereas Ernie hadn't done very well. Ernie listened to Emily and Sarah discuss their test results.

Suddenly, he shouted out 'Silly Sarah, silly Sarah

she's still reading baby books and she's bottom of the class for reading!' Poor Sarah began to cry at being picked on and she put her head down on her arms on the table top so that she could not see the other children looking at her. Then Ernie pointed to Emily and exclaimed loudly, 'Emily is just as dim. She can't do her sums and always comes bottom of the class.'

'You only know that about us because you listen to other peoples' conversations Ernie.' retorted Emily. 'You should mind your own business.'

Now Ernie could have offered to help Emily and Sarah with their reading and sums but instead he had chosen to be nasty and embarrass them in front of the whole class.

It so happened that Pinky had gone into school that day to help the children with their reading. She was sitting in a corner of the classroom helping a little girl when she looked up sharply at Ernie and thought what a horrible boy, listening to other peoples' conversations and then telling everyone what he had learned was definitely not nice. She decided that the next time she went into Ernie's classroom to help children with their reading she would keep a watch on him.

Sure enough the next Monday morning, from her place in the corner of the classroom as she waited for the first child to read to her, she could see Ernie's ears twitching as he leaned forward at the table where he was sitting. He was deliberately listening to

James and Ethan who were whispering to one another. The teacher had not yet begun the work for that morning and the children were just getting out their Geography books. Pinky could see Ernie smirking to himself so he had obviously found out something he shouldn't have!

Pinky got up from her seat and went round the classroom checking that the children had the correct reading books with them. When she got to Ernie's table she brushed the tips of Ernie's ears with some magic powder that she usually used to make her extra large 'Grinning Gobstoppers.' As Pinky returned to her seat the teacher asked the children to turn to page 10 in their Geography books so that they could learn about the major oceans and seas in the world.

However, Ernie just could not concentrate. His ears were itching and feeling hot. He put his hands up to scratch them and to his horror he found that they were growing. Not only that they were very fluffy! He covered them with the hood on his jacket and asked the teacher if he could be excused. He charged out of the classroom door and as he got into the corridor, PING! PING! Went both his ears as they popped out of his hood.

Now Ernie could see his reflection in the glass door of the headteacher's office. His ears looked just like rabbit's ears and they were ENORMOUS! Just then the headteacher looked up and saw Ernie standing outside. She was shocked! What was Ernie doing with rabbit's ears on the top of his head? The naughty boy must have bought some fake rabbit's ears and stuck them on his head for a joke! The headteacher was called Miss Penny and she beckoned to Ernie to come into her office.

'For goodness sake Ernie! Take off those ridiculous ears and go back to your classroom! It was April Fool's Day two months ago, not today so you are not fooling me! Go back and get on with your work!'

Poor Ernie gulped and then replied, 'Please Miss Penny, these are my ears, I was just listening to James and Ethan talking and they just suddenly sprang up from my head.'

Now Miss Penny knew how Ernie had a habit of listening to other people's conversations because several parents had complained to her about Ernie's bad habits.

'Well!' she remarked. 'It seems to me Ernie that you are being punished for listening to what other people are saying. You really must stop this bad habit of yours. I think someone has put a magic spell on you! She didn't know how right she was!!

Miss Penny suddenly remembered about the Extraordinary Egnormous Easter Egg that had a magic wish in it. If she remembered correctly it was Mrs. Spinks who had made that egg and the magic wish. She thought it would be a good idea to speak to Mrs. Spinks and see if she could do anything to get Ernie's ears back to normal.

Leaving Ernie in her office, she went to Ernie's classroom and asked Pinky if she could come and speak to her about an important matter. Pinky followed Miss Penny to her office and was amazed when she saw the size of Ernie's ears. Really! Some of her magic powders were a bit too strong!

'Can you do anything about Ernie's ears, Mrs Spinks?' asked Miss Penny. 'I'm afraid that magic is not within my field of knowledge. I believe you know a little about magic don't you?'

'Well,' admitted Pinky. I do know a little about making

magic wishes but Ernie's ears are so big I don't know
if they can be magicked away!'
 'Please Mrs. Spinks,' begged Ernie. 'If I can come to
your shop after school? Could you make me a magic
wish so I can wish these awful ears away?'
 'Actually,' said Miss Penny hastily. I think it would be
a good idea for you to go with Mrs. Spinks right now
before your ears get any bigger.'
 Miss Penny telephoned one of the children's mothers
to come in to replace Pinky and Pinky set off for her
shop with Ernie walking dejectedly behind her. He
bent his enormous ears over, then put his hood up,
holding the ears flat with both hands.
 Now, Pinky had been so pleased with the first magic
wish she had made that she made it a sort of hobby of
hers to make wishes of different strengths. She went
into her storeroom and fetched an extra strong wish,
after all Ernie's ears were ENORMOUS!
 'Here you are Ernie,' she said. 'You can unwrap this
wish when you get home but first you must promise me
one thing.'
 'Oh, anything, Mrs. Spinks. Anything!' replied Ernie.
'Just so I can get rid of these huge fluffy rabbits
ears. I would feel awful if the other children saw
them. I do know though what you want me to promise.
That I won't listen to other peoples' private
conversations anymore and tell other people what I
have heard. I won't, Mrs. Spinks, honestly I won't.
Oh,' he moaned. 'I think they are still growing. How

dreadful!'

Well, Ernie's wish did come true! He unwrapped the wish straight away so that by the time he got home they were almost back to their right size.

The next day, back to normal, Ernie asked Emily and Sarah if they would like to go to tea after school at his house. They would have a scrumptious tea and then play games. Emily and Sarah were very pleased and couldn't wait to go. What, they wondered had happened to change Ernie into such a good friend!!

CHARLIE CHUCKIT

CHAPTER ELEVEN

Charlie lived in the village with his grandma. To help his grandma out, he did a newspaper round every day after school. However, instead of posting the newspapers through peoples' letterboxes, he just flung them from where he was sitting on his bicycle on the pavement at their front doors. Sometimes, the pages blew out and fluttered over the neighbours' front gardens. Sometimes, the pages got torn and couldn't be read properly.

Charlie earned himself the nickname of Charlie Chuckit!

The people whose newspapers Charlie delivered got very cross and complained to the newsagent, Mr. Printer. BUT, it was no good complaining! Even when Charlie was told again and again to put the newspapers through the letterboxes, he just couldn't be bothered.

Pinky had her newspaper delivered every day by Charlie and went out of the shop door to pick it up. It was a windy day and most of the newspaper had blown away.

'That's it!' she said crossly. 'I've had enough of this newspaper nonsense! Things are going to have to change!'

The next afternoon, Pinky waited outside her shop

and when Charlie came along on his bicycle, she said to him

'Just a minute Charlie! I've got a few Sticky Sherbert Sizzlers left and there are not enough to make up into a bag to sell. Would you like them?'

Charlie's face lit up and as he got her newspaper out of his bag, he replied, 'Yes please Mrs. Spinks. I love Sherbert Sizzlers, they are my favourite sweets. Oh, by the way, here is your newspaper.' he said as he handed it over to Pinky.

Yes, thought Pinky and for a change it's all there and it isn't torn. As Charlie rode away on his bike, he popped TWO of the Sticky Sherbert Sizzlers into his mouth. (Sticky Sherbert Sizzlers were even stickier than toffees).

'Mm, delightfully delicious,' commented Charlie. 'I love Mrs. Spinks's sweets. They have flavours I've never tasted before and you can suck these Sherbert Sizzlers for absolutely ages!'

Then Charlie put his hand into his newspaper bag to take out a newspaper but it stuck fast to his hand!

'What's going on?' exclaimed Charlie. He tried to get the newspaper off by shaking it, then tried to peel it off. But he couldn't shift it! He got another newspaper out with his other hand and that stuck fast too. Suddenly, the rest of the newspapers whizzed out of his bag and joined the sticky ones on Charlie's hands.

Charlie had to push his bike with his feet on to the

pavement and leaving it there he hurried to Mr. Printer's shop to show him what had happened.

Mr. Printer thought it was very funny and couldn't stop laughing. He thought it was worth losing a few newspapers, for he hadn't seen anything so funny for months.

'That serves you right!' he said. 'I've told you countless times to post the newspapers through the letterboxes, but do you listen? No! no! no! The best thing is for you to go home and DON'T COME BACK UNTIL THE NEWSPAPERS COME OFF!' Meanwhile, Pinky had picked up Charlie's bike and she put it into her garden shed for safe keeping. Then, she went to Mr. Printer's shop to tell him that she had Charlie's bicycle and that Charlie could come and pick it up the next day. (Pinky's magic rarely lasted longer than a day!)

Pinky stopped to chat to Mr. Printer who told her what had happened to Charlie.

'What a funny thing to happen,' commented Pinky innocently as though she had nothing to do with it!! 'But Charlie will chuck the newspapers at peoples' front doors and then they either get torn or blow away. Can't you find someone else to deliver your newspapers?'

'Well, I could.' answered Mr. Printer. 'But, Charlie does need the job of being delivery boy because he lives with his Grandma and she doesn't have a lot of money.'

'Uh, I see!' replied Pinky. 'I didn't know that Mr. Printer.'

But the next day, Charlie had taken the hint! He started to post the newspapers THROUGH peoples' front door letter-boxes instead of flinging the newspapers AT peoples' front doors. Also, he was afraid the newspapers might stick to his hands again!

Pinky was so pleased she called Charlie into her shop one day soon after and rewarded him with a BIG box of mixed sweets. WHICH sweets do YOU think were in the box? Well, I don't know and I wrote this book!! What I do know is that Charlie ate only a few of the sweets every day and they lasted him for simply ages. His grandma was pleased too because she didn't need to buy any sweets for Charlie!

The next morning, Pinky found a letter on the doormat at her front door. She sat down in her armchair and read the letter. It was from her friend who lived at the seaside, asking her to go and stay with her for a while.

Hmm, thought Pinky. I've been living here for six months now. I could do with a break and I'm sure Sidney could too. I don't think anyone will miss me for a couple of weeks.

But, she was wrong! Everyone missed her very much! And, when she returned, her magic would be needed even more. For lots of children would come to stay with their uncles, aunties, grandmas and grandpas in the summer holidays.

THEY WOULD DEFINITELY WANT TO BUY SOME OF HER, SUPERLICIOUS, SO DELICIOUS, YUMMY, SCRUMMY SWEETS. DON'T YOU THINK SO?

35261239R00038

Printed in Poland
by Amazon Fulfillment
Poland Sp. z o.o., Wrocław